Killer Caramel Cookie

Book One

in

Killer Cookie

Cozy Mysteries

By

Patti Benning

Copyright 2016 Summer Prescott Books

Author's Note: On the next page, you'll find out how to access all of my books easily, as well as locate books by best-selling author, Summer Prescott. I'd love to hear your thoughts on my books, the storylines, and anything else that you'd like to comment on – reader feedback is very important to me. Please see the following page for my publisher's contact information. If you'd like to be on her list of "folks to contact" with updates, release and sales notifications, etc…just shoot her an email and let her know. Thanks for reading!

Also…

…if you're looking for more great reads, from me and Summer, check out the Summer Prescott Publishing Book Catalog:

http://summerprescottbooks.com/book-catalog/ for some truly delicious stories.

Contact Info for Summer Prescott Publishing:

Twitter: @summerprescott1

Blog and Book Catalog: http://summerprescottbooks.com

Email: summer.prescott.cozies@gmail.com

And...look up The Summer Prescott Fan Page on Facebook – let's be friends!

If you're an author and are interested in publishing with Summer Prescott Books – please send Summer an email and she'll send you submission guidelines.

TABLE OF CONTENTS

KILLER CARAMEL
COOKIE

Book One in Killer Cookie Cozy Mysteries

CHAPTER ONE

"You know the drill by now, Lilah, so I'll leave you to it. I'm glad to have you back. Start by checking on table two. It looks like he could use more coffee."

"Thanks, Randall. I owe you one."

Lilah Fallon straightened her name tag, brushed a stray crumb off of her shirt, then reached for the coffee pot. The diner's familiar kitchen was bright and welcoming, and the smell of frying bacon permeated the air, making her stomach pinch. She had spent most of the last paycheck from her previous job on rent, and her fridge at home was dishearteningly empty. At least here she'd be able to throw herself together a decent meal during her break.

Lilah pushed through the swinging doors into the dining area and headed for table two. She recognized the man sitting there; he was a regular that she had served countless times over the past couple of years.

"Hey, Levi. Do you want another coffee?" she asked in her brightest voice.

"Yes, please." He glanced up at her and did a double-take. "Lilah? When did you start working here again?"

"This morning. I was pretty lucky. Randall said he needed someone to cover morning shifts, and he had me start right away." She poured coffee into his mug, and found herself eying the stack of waffles on his plate. Her stomach growled.

"How long has it been since I've seen you last? A couple of weeks? A month?"

"About that." She gave him a self-conscious grin. "The voice-over job didn't last long. I probably shouldn't have kept mixing up the ads for hemorrhoid cream and ice cream."

Levi chuckled. "It's nice to have you around again. You always tell the best stories."

"I'm glad I keep you entertained," she said with a laugh. "You just holler if you need anything else, okay? I'll be here all morning."

Lilah left the diner at noon with a full stomach and a doggy bag containing a second sandwich for dinner. It was a hot day, as most days in Vista, Alabama were, with a slight breeze that made the short walk home all the more enjoyable. The ability to wear shorts to work, she reflected, was a definite perk of being away from the corporate world. She might miss a few things about the fast paced job in Montgomery that she had left behind a few years ago, but the dress code was definitely not one of them.

She paused outside of her bright yellow house to get the newspaper and the day's mail. Her orange tabby, Oscar, was visible in the window, sunning himself on the sill. Lilah waved to him as she walked up to the front door.

"I'm home, you two," she called as she pushed her way inside, trying to keep a hold of her purse, doggy bag, newspaper, mail, and keys without dropping anything. "Winnie, Oscar, come here and get treats."

There was the sound of claws scrabbling against the wood floor as Winnie, her beagle, jumped up from wherever she had been napping and hurried into the kitchen to greet her. Oscar followed more slowly, as if determined to show more dignity than the dog did. Lilah reached into an owl shaped cookie jar on the counter and withdrew two small treats. The first she tossed to Winnie, who made a valiant effort to catch it. It bounced off her nose, and she ended up chasing the treat across the floor.

With the dog otherwise occupied, Oscar approached and rubbed against her ankles, purring loudly. Lilah bent over and offered him the second treat, which he sniffed for a second before delicately taking it from her fingers. She smiled and stroked his back before straightening up to put her sandwich in the fridge and go through the mail.

Once she had put her bills into a pile to be ignored until her first paycheck from the diner, she poured herself a cold glass of lemonade from the fridge, pulled her brunette hair down from the tight ponytail it had been in for work, and settled down at the small round table in the kitchen to peruse the local newspaper, *The Vista Journal.* The upcoming Arts and Crafts Festival had made the front page. Lilah smiled to see her friend and neighbor, Margie Hatch, featured in the photo of last year's festival. She took a moment to read the article, then turned the next few pages over until she reached the ads section.

One ad in particular caught her eye. It was a local help wanted ad from the hair salon, offering a starting position with decent wages. An image of herself in a black stylist's apron putting the final touches of hair spray on a celebrity's up-do flashed through her mind. She didn't have much experience in cosmetology, but the ad said that they were willing to train the right person. There was no telling where this might take her, she thought with excitement. A whole new world of success and fun was at her fingertips. All she had to do was turn her resume in and hope for an interview. After some liberal use of the internet, she would practically be a hair care expert.

Excited by the prospect of her new career, Lilah took her lemonade outside and sat on the rocking bench by her front door while Winnie sniffed around. She really couldn't believe that she hadn't thought of working at a salon before. She loved talking to people, and she had always enjoyed playing with her friends' hair when she was a kid. The prospect of smelling like shampoo and conditioner when she got home from work, instead of bacon and sausage, was a good one too.

When it came down to it, she couldn't think of a single bad thing about being a hairdresser. Not like working as a voice-over actor, where people were always on her about pronouncing a certain word correctly, or criticizing the creative comments that she liked to add to the script. And what had she been thinking when she had taken that landscaping job for that rich guy? She had never been good with gardening tools. She should have known that trying to use the electric trimmer to sculpt the hedges would end in disaster. Compared to some of the jobs that she had done, working at the salon should be a walk in the park.

Lilah heard the screen door to her neighbor's house slam shut and saw Winnie's ears perk up. The beagle trotted across the yard, her white tipped tail wagging. The soon-to-be hairdresser turned to see an older woman approaching across the grass.

"Good afternoon, Lilah. Are you back from work already, or haven't you started yet?"

"Hi, Margie. I got back about half an hour ago. Randall let me begin right away," Lilah explained as her friend bent down to greet Winnie.

"That's nice of him," Margie said. "I came over to ask you if you would like to have dinner at my house tonight. Seeing as you have the rest of the day free, you're be welcome to come over a little bit early and help me make some cookies for the Arts and Crafts Festival."

"I'd love to, Margie, thanks. I've got to warn you though; I've never really spent much time baking."

"Don't you worry about a thing," her friend said with a warm smile. "You can learn as you go. I'll send you home with a few of them, so it will be worth your while."

"Thanks. I'm looking forward to it."

Lilah watched as Margie made her way back across the yard and into her house. After calling Winnie back, who had tried to follow her, she finished the last drops of her lemonade, got up, and went back inside to begin researching everything she could about the world of hair.

CHAPTER TWO

A few hours later, her mind stuffed to the brim with new knowledge about hair, Lilah brushed out her own hair, grabbed her phone, and said a quick goodbye to Winnie and Oscar.

"I'll just be over at Margie's," she told them. "Holler if you need something."

Bending over, she planted a kiss on the top of the beagle's head, then let herself out the front door and began the short walk across the grass. She was only a little surprised to see a car that she recognized sitting in her friend's driveway.

"Hi, Lilah," Reid said as she walked up the steps to the porch. "How are you?"

"Okay," she said, shifting awkwardly on her feet. He was crouched in the entranceway, a toolbox by his knee. There was no easy way around him. "What are you doing?"

"Margie asked me to come by and fix her screen door. I'm just about done." He tossed a screwdriver into the toolbox and stood up. "How is that voice-over job going?"

"I got fired."

"Oh." Reid fell silent, as if not quite sure what to say, then began fiddling with the door again. "Sorry to hear that."

"It's fine. I'm back at the diner for now." She decided not to mention the job at the hair salon; in the off chance that it didn't pan out, she didn't want to have to explain it to him.

At that moment, Margie appeared at the door, all smiles. "Oh, Lilah, you're here. I think Reid was just finishing up. Why don't you come in? And are you sure you don't want to stay for dinner, Reid?"

"Sorry, Margie, but I can't. Maybe next time." Reid picked up his toolbox and open and shut the screen door experimentally. "She's all fixed up. Let me know if you need anything else."

Lilah watched as he walked down the porch steps, toolbox in one hand, his sleeves rolled up to the elbows. Muscles flexed under the tanned skin of his forearms, and his dark hair was impeccably styled even after showing off his handyman skills in this heat. He was attractive, she would never deny that, but he was also everything she was trying to stay away from. She had the sneaking suspicion that Margie was trying to set them up, but when she glanced back at her friend, the older woman was smiling innocently.

"Ready to get to baking?" she asked.

"I am, if you are," Lilah said. "Lead the way."

Margie's kitchen reminded her of her grandmother's. It was chalk full of cookbooks and spices, with pots and pans hanging from hooks over the sink. It perpetually smelled of something delicious, and today was no exception; dinner was simmering away in the crockpot. The room was a warm place that she immediately felt at home in.

"What are we making today?" she asked as she walked over to the sink to wash her hands.

"I was thinking cookie cups. Chocolate chip with some sort of chocolate pudding filling, and sugar cookie with a fruit jam filling."

"Wow. Both of those sound amazing," Lilah said. "Where do we start?"

"We'll make the sugar cookie dough first, because it has to chill before we start using it. I've already got most of the ingredients out, but we'll need to open a new bag of sugar. Do you think you could get it down for me? Check the cupboard above the microwave. My hip's acting up, or I'd do it myself."

"Of course," Lilah said, dragging the step stool that her friend indicated over to the correct cupboard. She climbed up and opened the doors, spotting a couple of bags of sugar and flour, plus some unopened spices and cans. A can of pumpkin pie filling caught her eye. She licked her lips. Pumpkin pie was her favorite. It was too bad that they weren't making pie today. *That* was something that she would definitely be on board with.

An idea struck her as she grabbed one of the unopened bags of sugar. "Say, Margie, have you ever made pumpkin spice cookies before?"

"I can't say that I have, but they sound like they'd be good," her friend replied. "Do you want to give them a go? I'm not sure if I have all of the ingredients..."

As Margie fretted around the kitchen, making sure everything was ready for their baking adventure, Lilah picked up a cookbook that was laying out on the counter and flipped through it. It was filled with tasty looking desserts. She turned the page to see a caramel flavored cheesecake that looked decadent.

"Hey, Margie, if we make pumpkin spice cookies, could we try to do something like this for the filling?" She tilted the cookbook for her friend to see. "A pumpkin caramel cheesecake cookie sounds delicious, doesn't it? It would go well with the season, too."

"Sure, we can try whatever you would like, dear. I think I've got everything we'll need. Shall we get started?"

Under the older woman's direction, Lilah tied an old apron around herself and began combining the dry ingredients for her pumpkin spice cookies. Flour, baking powder, baking soda, and, to her surprise, salt, all went into the bowl together. She thought it seemed a little counter-intuitive to add salt to something that was supposed to be sweet, but trusted her friend's guidance. Margie often brought over baked goods, and they were always delicious, so she figured her friend must know what she was doing.

Once the basics had all been measured out and poured into the glass mixing bowl, Lilah peered at the row of spices that Margie had lined up next to their cooking station.

"I don't see pumpkin pie spice here," she told her friend. "Could you not find any?"

The older woman chuckled. "It's not just one spice, Lilah. It takes a mixture of spices to get the traditional pumpkin pie flavor, and I've got everything we need right here. See? Here's allspice — smell that, it's good, isn't it? — and nutmeg, cinnamon, and then just a dash of ginger. Now, you mix that all together, and I'll open that can of pumpkin."

The dry mixture smelled quite good indeed — just like Lilah thought pumpkin pie should smell like, in fact. She was impressed by how easily her friend seemed to remember all of these recipes. She hadn't even seen her check the cookbook once.

They mixed together the pumpkin pie filling, eggs, vanilla, sugar, and butter next, then Lilah stirred while Margie slowly added in the dry mixture. In what seemed like no time at all, they had cookie dough of the perfect consistency that smelled just like a pumpkin pie.

"That was easy," the newly converted baker said in awe. "I've had most of these ingredients all along. I can't believe I never thought about trying to make my own cookies before." That's what she got for spending most of her life so entrenched in the corporate world, she thought. She had missed out on a lot before she took the time to step back and smell the roses... or in this case, the pumpkin spice.

"We'll chill this dough for a bit while we get the plain sugar cookies done, then we can start baking," Margie said, covering the ball of dough with plastic wrap and putting it in the freezer.

"Why do we have to chill it?" Lilah asked.

"It makes it easier to work with," her friend explained. "It will hold its shape when we bake it better, too. It won't need long, though. You'll be able to taste your pumpkin cookies in no time."

They spent the better part of the next hour making the cookies. By the time the first batch was done and ready for her to try, Lilah's stomach was growling. The kitchen smelled even better than before, if that was possible, but it was also sweltering. She was relieved by the time she finished squeezing the last of the caramel cheesecake filling into the final pumpkin cookie cup and finally got the chance to pour herself a glass of cold iced tea from Margie's fridge and sit down.

"You really had a great idea, to make these cookies, Lilah," her friend said. "I think they need something sprinkled on top, though, don't you?"

"Like what?" she asked, standing up again.

"Something to tie the flavors of the cookie together with the filling... how about some cinnamon and maybe some crushed pecans?"

Lilah agreed that all of that sounded very good. It didn't take long for the two women to arrange the first batch of cookies on a platter, sprinkle the spice and crushed nuts over the pumpkin ones, and finish cleaning up the mess that they had left behind. At long last, Margie took two small plates down from the cupboard and put a pumpkin spice cookie cup on each of them.

"I think we've earned some dessert before dinner, don't you?" she asked, putting one of the plates at the table in front of Lilah and sitting down across from her with the other one.

Lilah picked up the cookie cup and took a tentative bite out of it, her eyes widening in shock. Was it really possible that something that she had made had turned out this good? She took another bite. Yep, she decided. Definitely possible.

"Mmm, I'm glad you came over to help, Lilah," Margie said. "This pumpkin spice idea of yours turned out well. It has a lot more pizazz than the cookies I was originally going to make."

"You're the one that told me how to do everything — I just had the idea," she replied. "I really enjoyed baking with you today. Next time you need help, let me know."

"I'll make sure to tell you," her friend said. "Now, I want to hear how you're doing. You holding up okay after losing your dream job?"

"I've decided that being a voice-over actress wasn't actually my dream job," Lilah said. "It was just... an interesting detour. I've found what I really want to do. The salon in Vista is hiring..."

With that, she began telling Margie everything that she had read about hair and life as a hairdresser. Tomorrow morning, she was planning to go to the local library and print off a resume. With any luck, she would be hired within the week.

PATTI BENNING

CHAPTER THREE

After turning in her — rather extensive — resume and doing an on-the-spot interview, Lilah waited an anxious twenty-four hours before getting a call back. She nearly jumped for joy at the news that she had gotten the job.

"When should I start?" she asked.

"Can you be here tomorrow, just before one?"

"Sure thing! Thank you so much." She hung up the phone, reflecting on how lucky she was, and then realizing that she had only a day to break the news to Randall that she would be quitting again so soon. He would understand… probably.

Walking into the hair salon on her first day of work was everything that she had dreamed it would be. A blast of air conditioning enveloped her as she came through the doors, accompanied by an array of scents from various hair products. Lilah could easily envision herself with a client, blow-drying a head full of silky hair.

"Lilah Fallon?" asked a woman with luscious red hair who was a few years older than Lilah, maybe even into her mid-forties.

"That's me," Lilah told her brightly. "Are you Gwen Foley?" She thought she recognized the woman's voice as the one from the phone call telling her that she was hired.

"I am. It's nice to meet you in person. Kristie had a lot of good things to say about you. It's wonderful that you were able to start so soon. I know she's eager to take some time off before her baby comes. Well, are you ready to get started? Today's a busier day than usual. With the festival coming up, everyone wants to look their best."

"I'm ready. Where do I start?" she asked, following her new boss over to one of the stations. She eyed the scissors there, wondering if she might get a chance to cut someone's hair on her first day.

Gwen eyed her for a moment, evaluating her. "Let's begin with shampooing," she suggested at last. "We'll go over scalp massage techniques, and I'll teach you about the different products while you observe me do a few washes. Then, we'll let you try one yourself."

"Sounds like a plan," Lilah said, eager to get started.

Her first day at the salon went off without a hitch. Gwen told her about all of the different types of shampoos and conditioners that they used, and showed her how to massage the products onto the scalp. The first time she was allowed to wash someone's hair by herself, she even got a compliment from the client on how gentle she was.

Feeling a glow of happiness deep inside her, and certain that she had finally found her true calling, Lilah volunteered to stay late and help clean up just so she could pick Gwen's brain for a little while longer.

"See you tomorrow," she called when she was on her way out the door at last. She was so focused on thoughts about her new job, that she nearly bowled her best friend over as she turned to walk down the sidewalk towards home.

"Whoa," Val said, putting an arm out to steady her. "Where are you off to in such a hurry?"

"Just on my way home. What about you? What's in all of those bags?" Lilah asked.

"Oh, just odds and ends for the art festival. Plus some books I need to drop off in the library's donation box. Margie roped me into that one."

Valerie Palmer was her old college roommate and current best friend. She was always knee-deep in whatever festival or activity was happening next in Vista, and usually tried her best to get Lilah involved, too.

"Do you need help carrying anything?" she asked her friend. "I could drop the books off at the library for you. I pass it on my way home."

"Oh, would you?" Val asked. "That would help a bundle. Thanks, Li'." She dumped a heavy paper bag into Lilah's arms. "I owe you one. Stop by the boutique sometime and pick out something nice for yourself. Stop and have a chat while you're at it. We don't see each other enough!"

With that, Valerie hurried off, and Lilah staggered under the load of books in the opposite direction. She was already halfway down the street when she realized that she had completely forgotten to tell her friend about her new job. She turned, but Val was long gone. Deciding to give her a call later, she continued on, wondering just how many books her friend had managed to find this time around. If she had to guess, she would have said a million.

At home, she took a short breather during which she filled up Winnie's food bowl, opened a new can of cat food for Oscar, and changed into more comfortable clothes. Still in a good mood from the first day at her job, she decided to go for a run. Her cupboards were still discouragingly empty, so on her way back, she planned to swing by the diner for dinner.

She set off towards town, the streetlights just beginning to come on. It was a pleasantly cool evening, which made running much more pleasurable than it had been earlier in the year. She quickly found her stride, her tennis shoes slapping the concrete of the sidewalk rhythmically. She lost herself in her thoughts, most of which involved her ambitious plans for the future.

She passed a few other people out for an evening stroll, but she was a good two miles into her run before she saw someone that she recognized. Reid. He had just turned the corner, and was looking down at his phone. He hadn't seen her yet. Lilah considered her options; she could keep going towards him, and likely be drawn into yet another conversation where he asked her about things that she didn't want to talk about; she could dodge across the street, which would work just fine if she wanted to get run over; or she could turn and take off in the opposite direction, back towards the diner and home.

Since the third option was the only one that didn't come with an awkward encounter or possible death, that was the one that she opted for. Performing what she thought was a very graceful move, she spun around mid-stride and started running back the way that she came. She thought, for a moment, that she heard someone call out her name, then decided that it had just been the wind, and forced herself to run even faster for good measure.

Lilah pushed her way into the diner a few minutes later, and closed her eyes with pleasure as the cooler air washed over her. She was glad that Randall's ancient air conditioner was still managing to chug along, despite being held together mostly with duct tape and good thoughts. Taking a seat in a booth by the door, she gave the waitress who brought her a cup of ice cold water a grateful smile.

"Thanks, Kate," she said. "You're a life saver."

"I didn't think I'd be seeing you in here for a while," the younger woman said. "You just quit yesterday, didn't you?"

"Yeah, but Randall understands," Lilah said. "Working here was only ever supposed to be temporary."

"I guess." Kate twirled a lock of her springy black hair around her finger. "What can I get ya? The special tonight is a Swiss mushroom burger with caramelized onions and steak sauce. And bottomless house fries."

"I'll take that. Thanks, Kate."

Feeling euphoric from her run and her awesome day at her new job, and a bit lightheaded from hunger, Lilah was happy to sit back in her booth and relax while she waited for her order. Her gaze traveled around the room, seeking out familiar faces. There was Marie Motts, who worked at the local country store, along with her son, Greg, who was about Lilah's age and worked at the local machine shop. A blond woman that she didn't recognize was sitting with them. She considered walking over to say hi, but decided against it — she was still sweaty from her run, after all.

Lilah took another sip of her water, then pulled out her phone to check her bank account. It was a good thing that she still had some tips from her last day at the diner, because her account was running near empty. Her job at the salon had really better pan out, because if it didn't, then she was going to have to start making some serious lifestyle changes.

34

PATTI BENNING

CHAPTER FOUR

Refreshed and ready for work, Lilah walked into the salon the next day itching to get to going. She was excited at the prospect of being able to work with more clients on her own today. Gwen had seemed so pleased with her skills the day before, and she was determined to do just as well, if not better, on her second day.

"Ready to get started?" her boss called over to her. "You can begin by shampooing Ms. Hawning's hair, while I finish up with Teri here."

Gwen already had a client in the chair, a pretty woman with light brown hair that Lilah assumed was Teri. There was another woman sitting in the waiting area, the same blond woman that she had seen at the diner the night before, in fact.

"Hi," she said with a smile. "I'm Lilah."

"Ellen Hawning," the woman said. She paused and looked expectantly at Lilah.

"Nice to meet you. If you'll follow me over to the sinks, I'll get you set up for a wash."

The other woman kept looking at her for another moment, as if waiting for her to say something else, then gave a sigh and stood up. "Very well."

Lilah led her towards the back, where she got her settled in one of the chairs by the sinks. She rolled up a towel and put it under the woman's neck, anxious to ensure that her client would be comfortable.

"Tell me if it's too warm or too cold," she said as she turned the water on.

She began wetting down the woman's hair, careful not to catch any of the strands on her fingers. Being as gentle as possible, she began massaging some of the salon's best shampoo into Ellen's hair. Working from her scalp all the way down to the tips of her hair, she made sure she didn't miss any of it. This client would walk out of the salon with the cleanest, softest hair imaginable.

"How much longer do you think you'll be, Gwen?" she asked as she began to rinse the suds out of Ellen's hair.

"Oh, another forty-five minutes to an hour, tops," her boss replied. "The highlights have to set, then I've still got to brush and style her hair."

Ellen gave another annoyed sigh. Lilah looked down at her, feeling bad. She probably wouldn't want to wait another hour to get her hair done either, if she was in the other woman's position.

"I'll do a special deep conditioning treatment for you while you wait, if you'd like," she suggested.

"Okay," Ellen said. "Do what you want."

Lilah grabbed the bottle and squirted a generous amount of the conditioner onto her palm. It was dark red, and smelled strongly chemical. From what her boss had said the day before, this professional conditioner was almost magical, able to bring lasting moisture to even the driest hair.

She began to work it through her client's hair, massaging her scalp and slowly working it down to the ends. After dragging her fingers through to make sure there weren't any tangles, she pinned Ellen's wet hair up, put a plastic cap over it, then parked her under a hair dryer, where she would sit for the next forty-five minutes while waiting for her turn with Gwen.

Lilah cleaned up her station while she waited, noticing that the two women in the chairs seemed to be trading nasty looks at each other. Was it just because they had been double booked, or was there another reason that they didn't like each other? She found herself watching them instead of cleaning, and quickly forced herself to focus on her job instead. She wasn't here to people watch; she was here to work.

It was nearly an hour before Gwen finally nodded to Lilah and told her that she could get started on rinsing the conditioner out of Ellen's hair. "I'm just about done with Teri," she said. "Make sure you rinse out the conditioner very well. If you leave any in, it will make her hair heavy and greasy looking."

"My hair has to be perfect," Ellen said, sounding concerned.

"Don't worry," Lilah assured her. "I'll rinse all of the conditioner out of it. You just sit down at the sink again and relax."

She rolled up a fresh, dry towel and settled Ellen's head down, taking some time to heat the water up to the right temperature before taking off the plastic cap. Humming to herself, she began to rinse the conditioner out. She rinsed. And rinsed. With a frown,

Lilah turned up the temperature of the water a bit more and began rubbing the other woman's hair with her fingers. For some reason, the red conditioner just didn't want to come out. Had she let it sit too long?

Beginning to feel concerned, she put the faucet head down and picked up the bottle of conditioner, looking for directions. What she saw made her heart skip a beat.

"Um, Gwen?" she said tentatively. "Could you come here for a second?"

"What's going on?" Ellen asked, looking up at her with a panicked expression.

"It's going to be all right," Lilah said. "Just... Gwen, I really need you!"

Her boss put down her brush and hurried over to the sinks. She gave her employee a quizzical look, then looked down at Ellen.

"Oh, my goodness," she said, going pale.

"I think... I think I used hair color instead of conditioner," Lilah said weakly. She and Gwen both stared down at their client in horrified silence. Ellen's beautiful blond hair was now bright red.

41

Teri, who had turned in her seat, half of her hair still up in curlers, started snickering when she saw the other woman's disastrous coloring. Ellen sat up like a bolt and started patting at her head, as if she would be able to feel the dye. She pulled a strand of hair in front of her eyes, gasped, then stood up and rushed over to a mirror, dripping pink drops of water all over the floor.

"What... what did you do?" she shrieked. She spun on Lilah. "How could you do this? Are you trying to sabotage me?"

"I didn't mean to! I promise, it was an accident. I thought I was using conditioner." She turned to Gwen. "You can wash it out, right?"

Her boss was shaking her head, looking mortified. "I can't wash out that dye, Lilah. It's semi-permanent, and will fade out on it's own over a few weeks."

"Can you color over it?" Ellen asked, touching her hand to her wet locks as she looked at herself in the mirror once more. "Just bleach it, or something. I need my blond back."

"Ellen, I'm sorry, but that dye sat on your hair for almost an hour. It would take a lot to bleach it out, and when I got done, your hair would be like straw. I hate to say it, but if you don't want to wreck your hair, you're going to have to wait it out. If you come back in a few weeks after it has faded some, then I may be able to do something."

"I wouldn't step foot in here again if you paid me. This is unacceptable. Your employee is incompetent. I'm going to sue. I'm going to make it so neither of you will ever be able to get another job in this town again."

"Good luck convincing anyone to listen to you, with that 'do,'" Teri said, still chortling over in her chair.

"Did *you* do this?" Ellen shrieked, turning on her. "Did you switch the bottles, or slip them an extra twenty under the table? Were you trying to get back at me? I'm going to make you pay for this, you little —"

"Ellen, I'm sorry, but I'm going to have to ask you to leave if you keep this up," Gwen cut in. "I'm truly sorry for what happened to your hair, and I can assure you we won't charge you for anything — I'll even give you a free cut if you want — but this behavior is completely inappropriate."

"I don't want a free cut! I'm never letting anyone from this salon near my head again."

Tears mingling with the water on her face, Ellen began to sob. She swiped her purse off the counter and hurried out of the hair salon, trailing pinkish water after her the whole way. The salon fell silent. With some trepidation, Lilah looked over at her boss. Gwen looked pale, tired, and most definitely angry.

"Get your things," she said in a toneless voice. "You're fired."

CHAPTER FIVE

"It's just like you never left," Randall said, patting her on the shoulder. "Your name tag's still in the drawer. Toss an apron on, and get to work. Kate will be in at three to relieve you."

With that, the old man went back to the stove and began turning sizzling strips of bacon over, as unruffled by her sudden reappearance as he had been by her quitting just as suddenly a couple of days ago. Lilah stood still for a moment, her brain still trying to process what had happened at the hair salon the day before. Thinking about it made her cringe. How could she have made such a horrible mistake? She felt so stupid. She would never be able to look Gwen in the eyes again. And Ellen, well… she thought that she would rather jump in front of a truck than come face to face with her.

Feeling numb, she grabbed an apron, tied it around her waist, then pinned her name tag onto her shirt. It was time to get to work; the last thing that she needed was to lose this job too. Hefting the pot of coffee, she pushed her way out through the kitchen doors, determined to put her best foot forward with this, just as she did with everything else.

When she saw who her very first customer of the day was, her mood sank even lower. Teri, the other woman from the salon, was sitting at the counter with a file folder and a stack of papers.

"Hi," Lilah said, hoping against hope that she wouldn't be recognized. "Would you like some coffee? This is real, and we've got decaf in the back."

Luck seemed to be with her for once. The woman seemed to be absorbed with her papers. When Lilah approached, she shifted the folder to cover them, and quickly said, "Real is fine. And I'm ready to order. I'll have a plate of sausage and hash browns. Thanks."

Normally she would have been upset if a customer treated her so brusquely and didn't even bother looking at her, but today she was grateful. She poured Teri's coffee, then hurried back into the kitchen to place her order. Maybe she would be able to get through this day without anything humiliating happening to her, after all.

When she brought out Teri's order, the woman behaved just as she had done before. She pulled the folder over the files, covered it protectively with her arm, and looked up warily. This time Lilah was sure that the woman was looking right at her, but if she recognized her, she didn't say anything. She put the plate of food in front of her, asked if she wanted anything else, and was more than happy to retreat to the kitchen once more when the answer was no.

She was glad that Teri wasn't making a big deal out of what had happened the day before. Despite her good luck, however, she was curious as to what exactly the woman was so focused on. Why did she keep hiding the papers whenever someone walked by? Lilah knew that it wasn't any of her business, but she was unable to help but glance over at them whenever she walked by to serve other customers. She finally got her chance when she was walking behind Teri back to the kitchen after wiping down a table. The front paper was a printed out picture of Ellen with her hands pressed to her newly red hair, and a horrified expression on her face.

Teri seemed to sense that someone was looking over her shoulder, because she snapped the folder shut an instant later. Lilah hurried back to the kitchen, wondering why on earth someone would be carting around pictures of Ellen like that. What had she stumbled into?

Lilah was still feeling sorry for herself the next day. She wasn't scheduled at the diner, and she didn't really want to see any of her friends. It would just be embarrassing to explain why she had been fired from yet another job. Margie would probably make her another meal out of pity, and Val… well, she loved Val, but her friend was notoriously outspoken. Right now what she needed was a nice, calm day at home with Oscar and Winnie. She would take a bath, try her hand at making some cookies on her own, and maybe have a glass of wine for good measure. She was bound to feel better tomorrow, after a day of pampering herself.

Deciding to get a start on the cookies first, with the vague idea of eating a plate of them in the bath while watching her favorite show on her phone, Lilah went into the kitchen and pulled out her one cookie sheet. It had come with the house, and up until now she had only ever used it to heat up frozen meals. She was glad to think that she was finally going to put it to some real use.

Trying to remember what ingredients Margie had used inn her sugar cookies — better to start out simple, she figured — she took down flour, sugar, and salt. Had her friend used baking powder or baking soda? Both? No, it couldn't have been both. Could it? She discovered that she only had baking soda in her cupboards, so that would have to do. Lilah realized that things might go more

49

smoothly if she looked up a recipe, but Margie had made it look so simple. Surely she could figure it out on her own.

She thought things started off well, but once she finished measuring out the dry ingredients, everything started to go downhill. First, she left the butter in the microwave for far too long, and instead of just softening it, she ended up with it completely melted. Since she hadn't put the stick on a plate, this meant that her microwave was completely flooded with butter. Then, she didn't have quite enough left to try again, so she ended up adding some milk to the dough. She figured they were both dairy, and it probably wouldn't end up tasting that different.

Once she finished mixing it, the dough seemed a lot more liquid than she remembered — more like batter, really. To firm it up, she added more flour. Eventually it got to a more dough-like consistency, but something still seemed off. At a loss for what else to do, Lilah formed a ball of dough with her hands and put it in the middle of the cookie sheet. She would start with one, and see how it turned out.

Ten minutes later, she dumped the whole batch of dough in the garbage can, then carried the bag outside and put it in the dumpster. The cookie had been bland, a bit too salty, and as hard as a rock. She had definitely gone wrong somewhere in the process; severely wrong by the taste of things. Next time, she promised herself, she would look up a recipe and follow it to a tee.

Her phone was ringing when she went back inside. She picked it up, only to find Randall on the other end.

"Lilah, can you come in today? The diner's busier than usual, with everyone in town getting ready for the Arts and Crafts festival. Kate can't handle it on her own, and my joints are acting up."

"I'll be there in a few," she said with a sigh. Her day wasn't going as she had planned in the slightest.

CHAPTER SIX

The diner *was* busy, and Lilah didn't have much time for self-pity between bussing tables and taking orders. She didn't really mind the extra hours, when it came down to it, and she definitely didn't mind the extra tips. Being busy worked wonders to take her mind off of the hair salon fiasco, and within her first hour there, she was beginning to feel a lot more upbeat.

Then Reid came in and her good mood began to fray. He made a beeline right for her when he spotted her, even though she was trying her hardest to look completely absorbed with the table that she was cleaning. Why couldn't he leave her be? He was just as handsome and well-dressed as ever, and here she was in her grubby apron with a dirty rag in her hand. Couldn't he see that she didn't want to talk right then?

Apparently not. When he reached the table she was cleaning, he leaned casually against the neighboring booth, with his hands in his pockets. He watched her in silence for a second, and Lilah wondered if he was expecting her to say something first.

"I'll be done with this table in a few seconds, if you're waiting to sit here."

"I'm just getting a coffee, I'll probably sit at the counter," he said. "I just wanted to check in with you. You were acting weird the other night."

Lilah looked up, confused. What was he talking about? They hadn't spoken since the evening that she had made cookies with Margie. She didn't think she had done anything weird then. Well, not weirder than normal, at least.

"You were jogging?" he prodded. "I was about to say hi, but you reversed direction so suddenly. I called out, but I don't think you heard me."

Oh… that. She winced. "I, ah, got hungry. I decided to head back and get dinner. Sorry I missed you."

"Don't worry about it. I was just concerned that something might have been wrong." He smiled at her. "I'll let you get back to work. See you at the festival?"

"I'll be there somewhere," she told him.

She breathed a sigh of relief when he walked away. It seemed that he hadn't heard about the salon catastrophe yet. She most definitely did not want to have to explain *that* to him. She was too embarrassed to even tell Margie. No, that wound needed time to heal before anyone began prodding at it. She was sure one day she would look back and laugh, but right now she felt more like crying.

Things didn't get any better when she saw who walked in next. Marie Motts walked in, with Greg and Ellen right behind her. Facing Reid was one thing; he was a decent guy, who just had terrible timing and a penchant for asking all the wrong questions. Ellen, however, was a completely different story. Lilah would have hidden in a dumpster rather than come face to face with the woman whose hair she had wrecked. Feeling like a coward, she backed away from the trio and slipped into the kitchen.

"Kate," she called out. "Can you take table, um…" she waited while Marie, Greg, and Ellen found a booth, "… table six? I need to… do something," she finished lamely.

Luckily, Kate was happy to help. She hurried out to take their order while Lilah busied herself with the dishes. This arrangement was only a temporary solution, though; it wouldn't have been fair to ask Kate to service all of the tables in the entire diner until those three left. She would just have to hope that she would be able to somehow slip by Ellen's table without her noticing when it came time for her to go and check up on her other customers.

She needn't have worried. Ellen, still sprouting a mane of red, was so involved in whatever she was talking about that she probably wouldn't have noticed an elephant walk into the room. She didn't even glance up at Kate when she brought their food, though Greg thanked the young woman sincerely. In fact, the more Lilah watched Ellen, the less bad she felt about her hair. As far as she was concerned, anyone who treated their waitress poorly deserved their hair to be accidentally dyed.

Feeling a bit better as she hurried by the table for a third time, a full tray balanced on her arm, Lilah couldn't help but to overhear a snatch of conversation. Ellen was sitting alone with Greg; Marie having vanished a few minutes before to use the restroom. The two were having an intense conversation, and reluctant redhead looked positively furious. Against her better judgment, Lilah deposited the plates at the table that she was supposed to be serving, then pulled a rag out of her pocket and began wiping down the already clean table behind Ellen, shamelessly eves dropping on the couple.

"My answer's the same, Greg. I don't want to move back to this podunk town, and I wouldn't be caught dead dating someone who runs a silly little toy store. Someone like me needs a successful man in her life."

"If it's money you're worried about, sweetie, you know I've got us covered. This is something I've always wanted —"

"It's not about the money!" Ellen hissed furiously. "You need to stop thinking about yourself so much. Quit being so selfish. Think about how this would affect *me*. After I finally get my good break, the media is going to be interested in everyone I know. I don't want the world hearing that the famous and beautiful Ellen Hawning is dating a *toymaker*."

"But, sweetie—"

"That's final, Greg. If you want to be with me, then you have to think of the bigger picture."

With that, Ellen took a sip of her lemonade, bit into her chicken club sandwich, and seemed confident that their argument was over. Lilah gaped at her, forgetting to even pretend to wash the table. To think she had felt *bad* for that woman. Now she was glad that she had accidentally colored the woman's hair. From what she had just heard, she had very much deserved it.

PATTI BENNING

CHAPTER SEVEN

The diner closed down early for the day so everyone would have a chance to go to the festival. Lilah, who was feeling much better about the fiasco at the salon, though she was still too embarrassed to want to talk about it, stopped off at home to let Winnie out and change into fresh clothes before walking towards town, where the festival was set up along Main Street. Both Val and Margie would have booths set up, and she was eager to see what her friends had brought to the Arts and Crafts Festival.

The entire town seemed to have turned up for the festivities. Everyone was in a good mood, and it wore off on her. She found herself smiling and admiring handmade items along with everyone else, the hair incident pushed to the back of her mind. She found Val's booth first, and spent a good half hour looking through everything her friend had brought from the boutique. The shop's full name was Val's Vintage Gifts and More, but most people in town just called it Val's. It sold everything from collectible figurines, to jewelry, to clothes. In fact, it sold pretty much anything that Val could get her hands on, which meant that its wares changed monthly, sometimes even weekly. Lilah loved the little shop, though she rarely found anything in it that she wanted to buy.

"How are things going?" her friend asked as she gazed at a display of gaudy, handwoven bags.

"Not bad," Lilah said, turning her attention to a rack of snow-globes.

"I heard about the salon," her friend said in a low voice.

"Oh." She put the snow globe down, and looked up to see her friend struggling not to laugh. "I don't want to talk about it. I feel terrible enough already."

"Oh, hun, don't worry about it. Ellen could stand to go down a peg. She's not a very nice person; if the same thing had happened to anyone else, I can guarantee you she would have been thrilled."

"I've been getting that feeling," Lilah told her. "I saw her at the diner earlier…"

She told her friend about Ellen's argument with Greg, and Val shook her head sadly. "Poor Greg. I'll never understand why he's dating her. I think *she's* in it only for his money — she needs someone to support her while she keeps trying for her big break."

"What is she? An actress?"

Val nodded. "She's been in a couple of commercials, and I think she was an extra in some film no one has ever seen. The paper ran a story on her a few years ago. It's a big deal when someone from Vista gets on national television, even just in a small way."

"Did you know her, back when you were going to school here?"

"She's a few years older than me, but I think we might have had a class or two together in high school. Come to think of it, she might have been in Reid's grade…" Val waggled her eyebrows. Her friend thought she was crazy for ignoring the handsome, successful businessman's advances. Lilah put her hands on her hips and glared until the other woman continued. "Anyway, from what I remember, she's always been full of herself. Don't feel too bad for messing up her hair."

"Even if she deserved it, I feel terrible for Gwen," she replied, sighing. "Ellen was so furious at her for letting someone as incompetent as me work on her hair that she threatened to sue."

62

"Well, if you feel that bad, you could always go apologize," Val told her in her usual no-nonsense manner. "She's got a booth with her hair products a little bit further down."

The last thing Lilah wanted to do was face her ex-boss, but she knew her friend was right. She definitely owed Gwen an apology. It would be embarrassing, but there was no point in putting it off, or she would just be thinking about it all day. With a reluctant goodbye to Val, she began trudging down the aisle, passing other booths full of interesting items, but forcing herself to ignore them until she had spoken to Gwen.

Just as her friend had said, the owner of the hair salon had a booth set up in front of her building. She was giving out free samples, coupons, and was even offering a drawing for a free shampoo and cut. Lilah waited for Gwen to finish speaking to another woman before walking up to the booth.

"Lilah," Gwen said, giving her a wary look. She didn't seem angry, so much as tired. "I'm sorry, but I can't give you your job back."

"I'm not here for that," she assured the older woman. "I came to tell you how sorry I am. I feel terrible."

She looked down, dejected. How could she have been so stupid? How could she have failed to notice that it was hair dye instead of conditioner?

"Thank you for apologizing," Gwen said after a minute of horrible silence. "I'm sorry I got so upset. What happened to Ellen's hair was just the last straw for me, I guess."

"What are you talking about?"

"Ever since that salon opened up at the mall in Bricksberg, business has been slowing down. If Ellen follows through with what she threatened and sues me, that would be the end of my salon. Though if she keeps up with spreading nasty rumors about my place, I might as well just shut my doors, even if she doesn't sue."

"I'm so sorry," Lilah said again, feeling even worse.

"I know you didn't mean to do anything wrong," Gwen said. "Don't beat yourself up. We all make mistakes. I just hope this isn't the end of my salon."

Though she was glad that she had apologized, it hadn't exactly made Lilah feel much better. She was still dragging her feet when she came up to Margie's stand. Looking at the beautiful array of cookies before her only made her feel worse as it brought back memories of her own failed attempt at baking. Couldn't she do anything right?

"Hi," she said dejectedly.

"Lilah!" Her friend exclaimed. "I'm so glad to see you. Look, almost half of your pumpkin caramel cheesecake cookies are gone already. People love them."

This made her brighten slightly. "Really? Wow, that's great, Margie."

"I'd love it if you came over and helped me out again sometime," the older woman said. "I bet you have even more great ideas. You're so much more creative than I am."

"I don't know about that…"

She told Margie about her failed batch of cookies, and to her surprise, her friend laughed.

"See? Much more creative. You tried to come up with your very own cookie recipe. All I do is follow old recipes."

"But I didn't see you looking at any recipes."

Margie tapped her temple with one finger. "I memorized them a long time ago. I think you've got the makings of a great baker, with some more practice. Let me know when you're ready to try again."

"Okay," Lilah said, brightening a bit. "Say, do you need any help with the cookie stand?" Helping Margie would take her mind off of other things, and she'd get to pick her friends brain more about cookies.

"Sure, another person to help count money and bag cookies would be nice," her friend said. "Come on back, and put on a pair of gloves. Grab a cookie to tide yourself over too, if you want."

She spent the next hour helping Margie sell cookies, and discovered that she loved talking to the customers. When one of them came back for seconds, or thirds, especially of the pumpkin cookies that she had come up with, it made her swell with happiness. What could be better than putting a smile on people's faces?

Lilah was in the middle of putting two pumpkin cookie cups and a butterscotch chip cookie in a bag for a middle aged man and his two daughters when she saw the first hints that something had gone wrong. A police car pulled slowly down the middle of the street, lights flashing. It parked in front of the town hall, not far from where Margie's cookie booth was set up, and an officer got out of the vehicle and went inside. A couple of minutes later, loudspeakers usually only used for emergency announcements crackled to life.

"Attention festival goers," a man's voice said, slightly distorted from the old speakers. "There has been a fatality. The festival will be closing down early. Law enforcement has requested that Main Street be cleared. Vendors, please pack up your booths in an orderly fashion and clear the street as quickly as possible. Thank you."

CHAPTER EIGHT

The second the loudspeakers crackled into silence, sound erupted on the street. People began talking, immediately asking everyone around them who had died. Phones were pulled out, as they called their loved ones to make sure they were okay. Lilah saw Marie at a booth across the street where she was selling coffee lower her cell phone with a shocked look on her face. She whispered something to her son, who was helping her, and he dropped the cup of coffee, not seeming to notice as the steaming liquid drenched his pants. Lilah got a sick feeling in her stomach even before Marie spoke.

"It was Ellen," she said, her voice raised enough to be heard across the street. The people around her fell quiet, and she spoke again. "Ellen is dead. Beth found her in the back room of the store."

They all knew that she was talking about the country store that she worked at. Main Street was almost silent as people took this in, then the volume began to rise again as people began asking what had happened. It seemed that Marie didn't have any information, though. In fact, she seemed pale. Lilah watched as she sat down heavily in her folding chair. Greg was still staring blankly into space, coffee dripping from his clothes.

Eventually more police cars showed up and the officers began to get the vendors and festival goers moving. They needed room to work without running anyone over, so Main Street had to be cleared. It seemed to take forever for people to pack up, but one by one the booths and displays were taken down and people started leaving. Lilah helped Margie pack up, and was about to accept the older woman's offer of a ride home when Val tugged at her sleeve.

"I've been looking all over for you," her friend said. "I just overheard Randall say he was going to open up the diner so people would have a place to talk. I'm going. Do you want to come with me?"

"All right," Lilah said. "I'll see you later, Margie." She waved goodbye to her neighbor, then followed Val back towards the diner.

"What do you think happened?" she asked.

"No idea," her friend said. "Maybe she slipped on something, and hit her head. Or maybe someone finally got fed up with her attitude and decided to teach her a lesson, only they went a little too far."

Lilah shuddered. "You don't really think that someone could have killed her, do you? I mean, it had to be an accident."

"I don't know. She wasn't ever very popular here," Val told her. "What sort of accident could she have had in the store? What was she even doing there, anyway? It was supposed to be closed for the festival."

"Maybe she somehow got locked in, and hurt herself trying to get out?"

Her friend shook her head. "I saw her helping Marie and Greg set up the coffee booth not too long ago. Whatever happened, happened recently."

No one at the diner seemed to have any answers either. The little restaurant was busier than Lilah had ever seen it before, and she was relieved when Randall didn't ask her to pick up a shift right then and there. Instead, she and Val got a pair of raspberry iced teas and sat in a booth with a couple of women that Val knew.

They tossed ideas back and forth, but no one had any real answers until Kristie, the young woman whom Lilah had been replacing at the salon, came in. One of the women at their table waved her over.

"Sit down, sweetie. What do you want to drink?"

"I'll just have a water, Aunt Diane. Thanks," she said, squeezing into the booth next to Lilah.

Diane got up to fetch a glass of ice water from Randall at the counter and came back to hand it to the pregnant woman. She waited until her niece had taken a sip, then spoke up.

"Are you all right, Kristie? You seem upset."

Lilah took a closer look at the girl next to her. She was pale, and the hand that was holding the glass of water was shaking.

"My friend Beth — Beth Preacher, you've met her, Aunt Diane — was the one that found the body," she said. She put the cup of water down and stared at it. "I just got off the phone with her. She's really freaked out."

All of the women at the table leaned in to look at the young woman.

"You spoke to her?" Val asked. "Maybe you can settle something for us, then. Was she murdered, or did she die in an accident?"

"She was murdered," the pregnant woman told them. "Beth said it looked like she had been hit on the head, and then stuffed into the back room. The police asked her not to give out any details, so I don't really know if I should be saying anything or not. I guess it was really bad, though."

Lilah felt cold. Ellen had been killed, and somehow that fact was made so much worse by the knowledge that she had died with that horrible hairdo. Every unkind thing she had thought about the woman seemed especially cruel now. No matter how horrible Ellen had been to her and others, she definitely hadn't deserved to die. She blinked and realized belatedly that the conversation had gone on without her.

"Who did it, though?" Val was asking. The women all looked expectantly towards Kristie, who shrugged.

"No idea."

"It could be anyone," Diane said. "She wasn't exactly popular around here, contrary to what she seemed to think."

"Wait, do you think it's someone from town?" Lilah asked. "Someone we know?"

"Could be."

At that moment the door to the diner opened again and a police officer walked in. The women watched as he walked up to the counter and spoke to Randall, who in turn pointed across the room, directly at Lilah.

"Ms. Fallon, do you have a moment?" the officer asked, walking over to their table.

"Um... I suppose?" It came out as a question. She glanced over at Val, who was watching with a concerned look on her face. No help there.

"Can you come with me?"

Kristie stood up so Lilah could slide out of the booth. She followed the officer towards the door, her heart pounding. What on earth did he want?

PATTI BENNING

CHAPTER NINE

"What is this about?" she asked after the door to the diner swung shut behind them.

"I'm Officer Eldridge with the Vista Police Department," he said. "I need to ask you some questions about your recent confrontation with Ellen Hawning."

"You mean the salon?" she asked. He nodded. "What do you need to know?"

"How did you know Ms. Hawning?"

"I didn't. That was the first time I had ever seen her."

He frowned. "What motivation did you have for putting the dye in her hair?"

Lilah stared at him. Did everyone in town know about that by now? Probably, considering how small the town was and how its residents loved to gossip. "I didn't have any motivation for it. It was an accident." She could tell from the skeptical look in his eye that he didn't believe her.

"Is it true that Ms. Hawning got you fired from your job at the salon?"

"Yes. Well, no. I mean, I got fired because I messed up," she said, feeling flustered. "I wouldn't say she got me fired."

"Where were you today between the hours of twelve and three?"

"At the diner, and then walking around the festival."

"Do you have anyone who can verify that?"

She did. Randall, Val, Gwen, and Margie had all seen her during those times. She gave him the numbers of the three women, then decided to ask a question of her own.

"Officer, am I a suspect?"

"Not as such. This is just a preliminary investigation."

She nodded, trying and failing to find comfort in his words. At least she had four people who would verify her alibi. Did he really think she had done it? If anything, Ellen had been the murderous one after the hair incident, considering how furious she had been. All Lilah wanted to do was forget about it and move on.

"Thank you for your time, Ms. Fallon," Eldridge said at last. "I may be in touch."

She nodded, and watched as he walked back inside the diner. It was with some relief that she saw him ask another person to come with him; it meant that she wasn't the only one that he was questioning today. Val turned in her seat and waved at her, urging her to come back inside, but Lilah shook her head. She wanted to get home, take a bath, and try her best to forget about everything that had happened in the past week.

She almost made it home, but just as she was walking past Margie's house, someone called out her name. Looking up, she saw Reid on her friend's porch. It looked like he was in the middle of fixing one of the steps. Lilah vaguely remembered her friend saying that one of the boards was rotted; it must have finally broke. She was glad that Reid was able to help the older woman so much, even though it meant that it was harder for her to avoid him. Reid had grown up in the home next to Margie's, the very house that Lilah was living in now, and Margie seemed to view him as the son that she had never had.

Raising her hand in a half-hearted wave, Lilah returned his greeting, then continued trudging towards her house. She only made it a couple of steps before she heard Margie's screen door open, and her friend stepped outside.

"Lilah, I thought I heard Reid say your name. Would you like to come in for a few minutes? I can whip up some sandwiches for us, and I'll pack up the rest of those pumpkin cookie cups for you to take home."

Lilah hesitated for a moment, but the tempting promise of free food was too much for her to resist. She walked up to the porch, accepting Reid's hand as he helped her over the broken step, and followed Margie into the kitchen. The sight of the half-full trays of cookies on the counter made her sad. Her friend had worked so hard to make all of them, and now wouldn't get a chance to sell most of them.

"Go on, sit down. I'll make us sandwiches. Rye or whole wheat?"

"Um, rye. But you don't have to make them, I can do it," she said, not wanting to take advantage of the older woman.

"Nonsense. You look exhausted. You've had a rough couple of days. Pour us drinks, if you must do something, then take a seat."

She did as she was told, pouring them each a glass of lemonade and then settling herself at the table. In no time at all, Margie set the most delicious looking sandwich she had ever seen in front of her. Melted Swiss, corned beef, and sauerkraut on toasted rye with just a dash of steak sauce. She realized just how hungry she was, having had nothing to eat but cookies since breakfast. The savory sandwich hit the spot, and was gone in just a couple of bites.

"Do you want another?" Margie asked.

"No, thanks." Lilah fell silent, gazing out the window. It was a sunny day, at odds with her mood, which was grey.

"What's wrong, Lilah? You know I'm here if you need to talk."

She did need to talk. Suddenly everything that had happened welled up inside of her, and she started sharing her fears and concerns with her friend. She felt better when she was done, though one thing was still nagging at her.

"Now Officer Eldridge thinks I might have killed Ellen. I'm so worried. I don't want to go to jail. I would never hurt anyone, not on purpose."

"I don't think you need to be concerned," Margie said gently. "Anyone who knows you would be able to tell him that you'd never do anything like that. He's probably following up on every lead he gets. I wouldn't take it personally."

"I hope so..." Lilah let out a long, slow breath. "I do feel better after talking. Thanks, Margie. And thanks for the sandwich."

"Not a problem, dear. You're always welcome here. Now, let me get some of those cookies for you. There's no way I'm going to eat them all, and I'd hate to see them go to waste."

A few minutes later, carrying a gallon zip lock bag with more cookies inside than she would ever be able to eat, Lilah finally walked through the door to her own house. She felt tired, but happier. She decided that Margie was right; there was no way she could be implicated in the murder. Ellen's death was sad, but it had nothing to do with her.

CHAPTER TEN

Lilah had just gotten into the bath when her phone rang. She glared at it, but it kept on making its cheery little tune, so with a sigh she put down her glass of wine and reached across the small room to grab it from the counter by the sink. Caller ID told her it was Val.

"Lilah, I just got off the phone with Greg. You'll *never* believe what he told me."

"What did he say?" she asked, sinking back into the bathwater. She had the feeling that this was going to be a long conversation — Val was one of the biggest gossips that she knew.

"Well, I called him to see how he was doing, you know, since he and Ellen were dating. I was worried, because he always seemed so devoted to her. You know, I thought he must have been totally smitten with her, otherwise why would he put up with so much? Anyway, he told that he was sad, but not as sad as he expected. He felt really guilty about this, but he told me that he felt like her death had freed him somehow."

Lilah frowned. "What? Did he really say that, Val? That's horrible."

"Well, I guess she was never very supportive of him. You know, he gave up everything so she could live her dream."

"Still, to say the death of someone you loved is freeing…" She shook her head. "I mean, she only died a few hours ago. Who even says something like that?"

"I've known Greg for ages. I think he feels just terrible about not being sadder about her death. Don't tell anyone what I said, all right?"

"I dunno… don't you think it's a bit suspicious, Val? His girlfriend is found dead, and he's relieved? I mean, they had just had an argument. I heard them in the diner. Shouldn't we tell someone at the police station about all of this?"

"Greg wouldn't hurt anyone," Val said firmly. "He's a good guy."

"If you say so," Lilah said, unable to hide the doubt in her voice.

They hung up, and Lilah was left with a sour feeling in her stomach. The more she thought about it, the more certain she was that Greg could have had something to do with Ellen's death. His mother, Marie, had worked at the country store for years, and it would have been easy enough for him to get the keys off of her, lure his girlfriend into the back, and kill her. Maybe he was tired of dating someone who pushed him around all the time.

She toyed with the idea of going to see Officer Eldridge with this new information, then decided against it for now. Val *had* asked her to keep it quiet, and her friend knew Greg much better than she did. She would just have to trust that her old college roommate knew best... for now.

The rest of her day was as relaxing as could be. She finished her bath, put a frozen lasagna in the oven for dinner, then curled up on the couch with Winnie and Oscar to watch old movies on television. She fell asleep early, halfway through a plate of Margie's cookies and an old western. When she woke up the next morning, the TV was still on, but the plate was empty. Winnie gave her an innocent, pumpkin-scented lick on the face, then rushed to the door to be let outside.

KILLER CARAMEL COOKIE: BOOK ONE IN KILLER COOKIE COZY MYSTERIES

Covering her mouth, Lilah gave a huge yawn and blinked in the early morning sunlight. She must have been tired last night, to fall asleep so quickly. She was usually something of a night owl. At least she had an early start on the day, though she had no idea what she was going to spend her time doing. She didn't have to go in to the diner, which would have been nice if she didn't so desperately need a paycheck.

"I guess it's as good of a day as any for some spring cleaning, right, Winnie?"

The dog wagged her tail at the sound of her name, evidently agreeing. Lilah let her back inside, fed her and Oscar, then decided to tackle the mess that she had left behind the night before.

It wasn't long before she was thoroughly bored with cleaning. Throwing her rag into the sink with the remainder of the dirty dishes from the night before, she considered heading into town, or maybe stopping by the boutique to see Val. Thoughts of her friend reminded her of the conversation from the evening before. She thought of Greg, and wondered if he really had killed Ellen or not. It was true that a lot of people hadn't liked the woman, but was there anyone else who held a grudge against her that could be motive for murder? She just didn't know. She hadn't grown up in Vista, like so many of the residents had, and she just didn't know enough of the answers to the questions that she had, but she knew who would. There was one man in this town who knew everything about everybody, and was almost as much of a gossip as her friend Val. Levi.

Levi Hayes was many things, and one of them was predictable. He almost always went to the diner for lunch, which meant he should be relatively easy to find. He had lived in Vista his whole life, so he would probably know plenty about Ellen, and he was always happy to talk to a friendly face.

"You want to talk about Ellen?" Levi stirred a pack of sugar into his coffee, then tapped his spoon against the edge of the ceramic mug before setting it down. "Join the club. That's all anyone in town is talking about."

"I didn't know her very well. I was hoping you might have some insight on who else would have had motive to kill her, since you know pretty much everyone in town," she explained.

"Oh plenty of people. Wait… you said who *else*. Do you have someone currently in mind?"

"Well, me," Lilah said, not wanting to betray what Val had said about Greg just yet. "Officer Eldridge questioned me yesterday.

He seemed to think that since the incident with her at the salon cost me my job, I might have had motive to do it."

"Did you?" he asked, raising his eyebrows.

"No! I can't believe you'd even say that, Levi. You've known me for how long? A couple of years, at least? I would never hurt anyone. Besides, what happened at the salon was completely my fault, not hers."

"I was just asking," he said. "I've known you for a couple of years, sure, but that's nothing compared to how long I've known most of these people. And I can tell you right now, plenty of people had reason to dislike Ellen. But I don't know if any of them had it in them to kill her."

"Well, obviously someone did. And chances are, it wasn't some drifter."

"You've got a point," he admitted. "Tell you what. I'll keep my ear to the ground. If I hear anything suspicious, you'll be the first to know. Consider it thanks for all that free coffee you've given me over the years."

CHAPTER ELEVEN

Her conversation with Levi hadn't exactly panned out any juicy hints at who the murderer — or murderess — might be, but despite that, Lilah had thoroughly enjoyed her first taste of detective work. An idea occurred to her as she walked back towards her house. Maybe she wasn't suited for the world of hair care, or voice acting, or countless other things, but she was positive that there was something out there that she would be a natural at. What if that something was detective work?

She envisioned herself dressed in a long, dark trench coat solving mysteries for the citizens of Vista. She wouldn't join the police force, no, she knew that she would never get through the long weeks of physical training — she loved running, but had always hated the gym and the pressure of having people judge her. But maybe as a private investigator, she could find her niche.

Lilah made a deal with herself then and there. If she could find out who had murdered Ellen before the police did, then she would take whatever classes she needed to become a private eye. She wasn't going to jump into her new career path with no idea what she was getting herself into, like she had done with the world of hair care. She figured that solving this case would be a good first step, to see if she was really suited to being a detective.

If she was serious about her potential new career, she knew that it meant she would have to suck it up and do something that she would rather not; question Reid. She didn't think he was the killer, but he had grown up with Ellen, so he might have some idea of who would have the motive to kill her. Lilah entertained the idea of asking him to meet her at the diner, but the last thing that she wanted was him thinking she was asking him on a date. No, Margie's house would work just fine for her purposes.

Her friend was all too eager to be of help. The older woman told Lilah that she was free to use her porch — with its freshly repaired step — for as long as she wanted, and she would even provide as much lemonade as they could drink. For once, Lilah was glad that she had let Reid pressure her into giving her his number; for the first time since he had put it in her phone, she used it to call him. He agreed to meet her as soon as he got off of work. As executive officer of the local machine shop, he worked long hours and was practically married to his job, which was just one more good reason for Lilah to keep spurning his advances. In this case, though, his devotion to work was a good thing as it gave her some time to get ready and figure out exactly what she was going to say to him.

"The two of you just let me know if you need anything else," Margie said, every inch the mother hen as she laid down the tray of cookies and lemonade. Winnie, whom Lilah had brought along for moral support, thumped her tail against the wooden slats of the porch. She was a fan of Margie's cookies, and had been begging her owner for more ever since she had finished that plate of them.

"You said you needed to ask me something about Ellen?" Reid said after the older woman went back inside.

"I was just, you know, wondering about her," Lilah said, suddenly forgetting everything she had planned on saying. Reid was looking especially handsome today, in a charcoal grey button up shirt. The top two buttons were undone, and she caught a glimpse of his muscular chest. She had the sneaking suspicion that he had changed before coming over, and had purposely picked out something that would show off his body. She doubted Reid ever did anything by accident.

"What about her?" he asked, arching an eyebrow and taking a sip of his lemonade.

"Well, did she have any enemies that come to mind? Anyone that might have wanted to hurt her?" She was on a roll now. It was easier to focus on her questions if she looked down at the cookies instead of up at him.

"Are you thinking of joining the police force next?" he asked with a chuckle. "Why do you want to know all of this?"

"Just curiosity," she said, giving him her best winning smile. He considered for a moment, then evidentially decided that his chances of actually going on a date with her at some point would be better if he complied.

"One person does come to mind," he said, fiddling with his glass. "Teri Moran. They never got along, and always seemed to have it out for each other from grade school onward."

"Why?" she asked. "What did Ellen do to her?"

"It wasn't one thing, exactly," he said. "But they always were into the same sort of stuff. They both tried out for all of the same plays, they entered all of the same contests… and Teri always came out on top. Ellen hated her with a passion. She tried to rub her limited

93

success as an actress in Teri's face whenever she came back to town, but Teri never seemed to care. It just made Ellen even more angry."

"Teri was at the salon the day I messed up Ellen's hair," Lilah said. "She was laughing at her. Ellen accused her of setting it up somehow, switching the bottles of conditioner and dye?"

"Were they?" She stared at him blankly, and he added, "Switched. Were they switched?"

"Oh." Lilah thought back to that horrible day that she had tried so hard to block from her memory. "No, I don't think so. Is that something that Teri would do?"

Reid shrugged. "They were constantly at each other's throats back in high school. I can't imagine that much has changed."

"It's been, what, nearly twenty years since they've graduated?"

"Those two woman would still have hated each other if it had been sixty years," he said. "Some things never change."

PATTI BENNING

CHAPTER TWELVE

Lilah's alarm woke her bright and early the next morning. She was bursting with energy, her thoughts still on her new plan to have a career as a private investigator. With two hours to spare before work, she decided to go for a run. It was early enough to be cool out, at least, and she wasn't likely to run into too many people that she knew.

She grabbed her headphones and her cell phone and started her favorite running playlist. Bouncing on her toes to the beat of the music, she spent a moment deciding which way to run, then decided to head towards town. She took off down the sidewalk, feeling light and free, focusing on nothing but the music and the ground beneath her feet.

Running had always been one of her favorite ways to clear her mind. Her thoughts seemed to wander, coming up with solutions to various problems without any actual effort on her part. So when she passed by the police station and the thought popped into her mind to go and tell Eldridge about Greg and his less-than-crushed attitude towards his girlfriend's death, she decided to go along with it. She was ninety-percent certain that withholding important information from a police officer was a crime, and she couldn't very well start off her career as a private eye with a black mark on her criminal record.

She let herself in the doors of the police station and told the woman behind the desk that she was there to see Officer Eldridge. Asked to wait, Lilah sat down in one of the uncomfortable plastic chairs, looking around the room in hopes of seeing a water fountain. No such luck. Maybe Eldridge would offer her a drink while they spoke.

After a few minutes a door on the other side of the room opened and Eldridge poked his head out. When he saw her, he gestured for her to get up and follow him, which she did. The hallway they walked down was windowless and smelled strongly of coffee. When they reached his office, he told her to take a seat.

"How can I help you, Ms. Fallon?" He was watching her closely, and the thought entered her mind that he was expecting her to confess.

"I know someone who might have had a motive to kill Ellen," she said. "Her boyfriend, Greg Motts."

He steepled his fingers and raised his eyebrows. "Tell me why you say that."

"Well, he told my friend that he was sad that Ellen was dead, but that it also felt freeing. And I saw them arguing not long before she was killed."

Eldridge nodded slowly. "I see. Who is this friend that you mentioned?"

"Oh, um, Val. Valerie Palmer." She hoped that her friend wouldn't be too mad about her giving this information to the police. It was a matter of safety, after all. If Greg was the killer, then he deserved to be in jail.

"Val. She runs the boutique store, doesn't she?"

Lilah nodded. "That's all I wanted to say. I should get going now. I've got work in a little while, and I jogged here."

"Wait just one moment," he said, holding up a finger. "I have to ask, did you really think coming in here and telling me all of this... this hearsay, would help you?"

"What?" she asked, shocked.

"If anything, this just makes you look more suspicious. Redirection is one of the oldest tricks in the book, but I don't think I've ever seen it done so clumsily."

"I'm not trying to redirect anything," she said, aghast. "I'm just trying to help."

"If that's the case, then I'll give you some advice. Back off. Don't get involved in police business unless you want to be slapped with an obstruction of justice charge. What we do can be dangerous, and we definitely don't need civilians getting in the way."

With that, he dismissed her. Lilah trudged back out of the building feeling defeated. She had only been trying to help. She wasn't trying to get in the way, or mess up their investigation. Was this what she could expect if she tried to break into the field of private detection? Would no one take her seriously? She began to jog slowly back towards home, the bounce in her step gone.

She had just let herself in her front door when her cell phone rang. It was Levi, calling to ask her to meet him.

"I've got news," he said. "I found out something about why somebody might want to kill Ellen."

He wouldn't tell her any more than that over the phone, though, so she offered to meet him at the diner before her shift began. It would mean getting there a few minutes early, but she didn't think that Randall would care if she used the place to meet with Levi before opening.

He looked excited when she saw him. He waited impatiently while she unlocked the doors, then led the way through the empty diner to a booth in the corner. She sat across from him.

"All right, what is it?" she asked. "I'm on the edge of my seat."

"Well, I did some digging, like I promised," he said. "Okay, being honest, I kind of stumbled onto this accidentally. I drove my niece to get her hair cut, and happened to overhear Gwen Foley talking to that assistant of hers… Kristie, I think it is. Anyway, they were talking about Ellen's death. Kristie was saying how horrible it was, but Gwen told her that she wasn't sad at all — in fact she was relieved, because it meant that Ellen couldn't sue her."

"She did tell me how worried she was about being sued and having to close down the salon," Lilah said. "She said that only a few hours before Ellen's body was found."

"And that's not all," Levi said grimly. "When she went into the back, I got on her computer, just to take a quick look through her files. The day of the festival, she canceled her last appointment of the day. I did some quick calculations, and it all adds up — with the appointment canceled, she would have had enough time to kill Ellen before setting up her booth for the festival, and no one would be the wiser."

Lilah sat back in her seat, her brain working in overdrive. It made sense, all of it. Gwen had a motive to kill her, and she would have had the time to do it without anyone noticing. Her salon was right across the street from the little country store. She could have been in and out without anyone noticing.

"Thanks for telling me this, Levi," Lilah said. "Poor Ellen. I didn't like her very much after she went off on me at the salon, but she definitely didn't deserve this." She took a deep breath and turned her mind to its next important task; deciding what to do with this information now that she had it.

KILLER CARAMEL COOKIE: BOOK ONE IN KILLER COOKIE COZY MYSTERIES

CHAPTER THIRTEEN

Her shift at the diner had never felt longer than it did that day. Usually she enjoyed her time there, and loved talking to the citizens of the small town, but today all she wanted was to get out of there as quickly as possible so she could tell her friends what she had learned. Luckily, Kate was on time for her shift, and Lilah was able to dash out the doors the moment her shift ended. She hurried home and let Winnie outside while she called first Margie, then Val and Reid. They had all helped her in her mission to figure out who the killer was, and they all deserved to hear this.

Less than an hour later, the four of them were sitting around Margie's kitchen table. A plate of marmalade cinnamon sugar cookies, still warm from the oven, was in the center of the table, and they each had a glass of ice water. No one ever went to Margie Hatch's house and left on an empty stomach.

Over the cookies, Lilah told them all what Levi had told her only a few hours ago. She added in everything she remembered about the incident at the hair salon, including Ellen's threats to sue, and also told her friends that Gwen had confided in her shortly before Ellen's body was found that she had been worried about being forced to shut her doors from the bad publicity.

"It all makes sense," she said at last. "If Ellen had followed through with that lawsuit, it would have meant the end of Gwen's salon."

Margie was nodding sadly. "You might be right, Lilah. Even if Ellen didn't end up getting any money from her, just the publicity would probably have been enough to do Gwen in. Nearly everyone in Vista knows who Ellen was — not many of us end up on national television, after all — and I think a lot of the ladies would have been persuaded to go elsewhere for their hair if our local star started badmouthing Gwen's place."

"It does seem like a pretty good motive to me," Reid said after careful consideration. "But you said that you spoke to her at the festival shortly before Ellen was found. Why would she still be worried about the lawsuit, if she had just killed the person responsible for it?"

"Maybe she was trying to cover her tracks," Lilah suggested. "She could have been trying to make herself look less suspicious. What do you think, Val?"

Her friend frowned, surprising her. Val had been the one person that she had expected agreement from. "I think… I think you might have been right the first time, Lilah."

"Huh?"

"Greg," her friend said simply.

"Now I'm confused. I thought you said Greg would never do anything like that. Now you think he's the killer?"

Val hesitated. "I'm not saying that exactly, but, well, he's been acting even more strangely. He called me just this morning to say that he had put a down payment on a space for that toy store he's always wanted."

"Ellen's only been dead for *days*," Lilah said, aghast.

"That's why I think you might have been right about him," the other woman said, nodding. "I mean, I tried to be understanding when he told me the truth about how he felt about her death, but he sounded *happy* on the phone this morning. He didn't seem curious about who killed her at all. He just said he felt a lot better than he had in a long time, like he could finally see the path forward."

"That's creepy." Lilah bit her lip and looked down at the half cookie remaining on her plate, deep in thought. When she had called up her friends, she had been so sure that Gwen was the killer. But if Greg was acting suspicious too, suspicious enough for Val to suspect him, then she was at a loss. Both of them had had a motive to kill Ellen. Both of them would have had the time to do it, and both of them had benefited from her death. But only one of them had killed her. The only question was, who?

She spent the rest of the evening alone at home, driving herself crazy by going over the crime again and again in her mind. She tried to remember every word that she had exchanged with Gwen, but nothing helped. The two days that she had worked for the woman hadn't really given her much insight into her personality or what she might be capable of. The one thing that she knew was that Gwen loved the salon. Lilah could guess that she would go to extreme lengths to keep it open... but would she kill someone for it?

Then there was Greg. She knew his mother, Marie Motts, some, but had hardly ever spoken to her son. From what she had gathered, he had been with Ellen for years. What would have made him snap now? Did it have something to do with that argument she had overheard? Once again, there was no way to tell. She just didn't have enough information about either person. As far as she was concerned, neither reason was a good one to kill someone. No matter how rude Ellen had been, she hadn't deserved to die for it.

"Well, Winnie, this is the real test, isn't it?" she said to her dog. "If I can't figure out who killed Ellen, then I'll know I don't have what it takes to be a private eye. But if I can, well, how would you feel about being my partner? You can sniff for clues, and scare off the bad guys if they try to hurt us."

The beagle wagged her tail and rolled over for belly scratches, which Lilah obediently provided. Oscar joined them, demanding to be petted as well. Her pets may not be able to help her solve the murder, but they did make her feel better, and that was just as important.

CHAPTER FOURTEEN

"Table five wants a bacon burger with no pickles and extra cheese," Lilah called back to the kitchen. Randall nodded to show that he had heard, then scooped a fresh batch of fries out of the deep fryer. It was a busy afternoon at the diner, and both of them were multitasking. It had been hours since she had gotten a chance to sit down, and her feet were aching. At least she got to spend most of her time out in the slightly cooler dining area, talking to the guests and gathering tips. She did not envy the older man his station at the stove.

"Order up, table three," he called out a minute later, and she hurried back into the sweltering kitchen to grab a plate with a club sandwich, fries, and coleslaw. Table three was a booth in the corner, more private than most of the others. There was one woman at it — Teri. She had brought that file folder with her again, and Lilah had been keeping a close eye on her. Was she still looking at something involving Ellen, or was she going over something different? She had been unable to tell, and didn't want to make a nuisance of herself and put the woman even more on edge.

"Here's your sandwich," she said, putting the plate in front of Teri. "Let me know if you need anything else. Would you like another soda?"

"No, thanks."

Lilah waited for a second in case the other woman was going to volunteer anything else, then finally made herself walk away. She had other guests to tend to, and tips to earn. If things kept going this well, then she might even be able to restock her kitchen this afternoon. She was eager to try making cookies again — this time while following a recipe.

It wasn't until nearly an hour later when Teri left and Lilah went over to wipe down the table that she noticed the manila folder was sitting on the booth seat. She froze, staring at the folder as temptation made her hands twitch. A quick look around showed her that the woman was nowhere to be seen. She wouldn't get a better chance than this to snoop.

Lilah picked up the folder, stuck it down the front of her apron, and quickly wiped down the table, eager to take a look at the files before Teri realized that she had left the folder behind.

"I'm taking my break," she said as she hurried through the kitchen on her way to the back door, where she would get some privacy. She didn't pause to listen for Randall's response.

Behind the diner was a small, worn out picnic table, chained to the side of the building. She wasn't quite sure about the reason behind the chains — who would want to steal a picnic table, and in Vista, of all places? Regardless, the table worked for what she needed; a quiet place to rest her feet and look through the file. Ignoring the lingering scent of cigar smoke from Randall's bad habit, she pulled the folder out of her apron and set it on the table. Bracing herself for whatever she might find inside, she opened it.

At first, she was a bit disappointed. She had half been expecting gruesome pictures of the murder scene, or maybe a written confession from Teri, who had made it to the top of her suspect list again. Instead she found what looked like a calendar, a printed out email, and a few photos of Ellen with her red hair, or making awkward faces. It was obvious that she hadn't been aware of the pictures being taken. Lilah examined them closely before setting them aside and turning her attention to the calendar.

It took her a moment to realize what she was looking at. This was a printout of Ellen's calendar. It covered the last few weeks, and the upcoming month. It showed every appointment she had, including the ill-fated one at the hair salon. It must have been printed out from her phone or computer. Had Teri had this the whole time? If so, it would have made it very easy for her to follow Ellen around and find a time when she could catch her alone.

She looked at the printed out email. It was a letter from a booking agency, sending their regrets that Teri had not been chosen for a part in a local commercial. At the bottom, Ellen's name was written in pen and had been circled over and over again, presumably by someone who was quite angry with her, judging by the indents in the paper. Had Ellen stolen a part in a commercial from Teri? If so, that would give Teri a motive, an especially strong one, considering their history. Lilah had no idea what the purpose behind the pictures was, but she was certain it wasn't good.

The more she looked at the contents of the folder, the more certain she became of what exactly it was that she was holding. This was evidence, once and for all, that Teri had killed Ellen. There could be no other explanation. Innocent people didn't just go carrying this sort of stuff around. Greg and Gwen had been leaps, guesses

— but this time she was sure. Teri was the murderer. She had solved it.

Bursting with excitement, she dug her cell phone out of her pocket and called Val. No answer. Frustrated, she tried the boutique next, and was sent directly to the shop's automated answering service. She glanced at her watch, and realized it was too early for Val to be at the boutique anyway. If she wasn't answering her cell phone, then that must mean that she was at her dad's lumberyard. She helped out there sometimes when she wasn't busy with her own store, and had been going there more and more often as her father aged. Lilah tried that number next, and was finally met with success when a receptionist answered and promised to put her through to Val's work phone.

"Val," she said when her friend finally answered. "I know who it was."

"What are you talking about?" Val asked. "I'm with a customer."

"I know who killed Ellen!"

"You do? Was it Greg?" her friend asked, lowering her voice.

"No, no. He's innocent. It was Teri." She quickly explained what she had found in the file folder. "It can't be anyone else. There's just too much evidence that points to her."

"Wow. I can't believe I'm saying this, but I think you're right. You should —"

A sudden ear-piercing shriek nearly made her drop the phone.

"Val? Val!" Lilah called, listening desperately for any sound from her friend on the other line. Nothing. The line was dead.

Desperate with worry, she stuffed the papers back into the folder and ran back into the kitchen. She told Randall that she had a personal emergency and had to leave immediately. He must have seen something on her face, because he didn't argue.

"I'll call Kate to cover your shift," he told her. "You go."

Not even bothering to remove her apron, she rushed out of the diner and ran across the street towards Margie's house. It seemed to take forever to cover that short distance Thankfully, her friend answered the door right away.

"Lilah?" she asked. "What is it? What's wrong?"

"Val's in trouble," she gasped. "Something happened... at the lumberyard... need car..."

Somehow the older woman managed to understand her through her ragged breathing. "Of course you can borrow my car, dear, but should you really be driving in the state that you're in? Is Val hurt? Shouldn't you call the police?"

"Eldridge won't listen," Lilah said. "He told me to back off from the investigation. He thinks I killed Ellen. I can't waste time with him... Val needs me."

Margie met her eyes, then nodded firmly. "All right. Here are my keys. Be careful, Lilah. I don't know what the pair of you have gotten yourselves into, but it doesn't sound good."

PATTI BENNING

CHAPTER FIFTEEN

Lilah tried dialing her friend's number again as she drove Margie's minivan towards the lumber yard, which was on the opposite side of town, near the machine shop. No answer, but she hadn't been expecting one. It still made her heart clench in fear.

Struck by a sudden, painfully obvious idea, she tried calling the lumberyard itself. This time, however, there was no answer. That was almost more worrying than Val not answering. What had happened to the receptionist? Had she been hurt too, somehow? She was beginning to dread what she would find when she got there.

She pulled into the parking lot just outside of the lumberyard's gates, which were locked and closed. A sign out front said *Out for Lunch* with a little paper clock promising that they would be open again by one. Lilah felt a surge of annoyance at the receptionist, who had taken her lunch break when Val could be hurt or dying in the yard.

"Calm down," she muttered to herself. Realistically, she knew that the receptionist probably had no idea that something was wrong with Val. She had just left on her scheduled lunch break, like always, having no clue that she was leaving her boss's daughter inside, probably bleeding to death somewhere.

Trying her friend's cell phone again to no avail, Lilah surveyed the fence surrounding the lumberyard. It was about six feet tall, though thankfully not topped with barbed wire. She could probably climb over it, if she had to, but she really didn't want to — she had never been very good with heights.

"Val?" she called, hoping her friend would make this easy for her and answer. Maybe she had just dropped the phone, and the scream that she thought she had heard had really just been some sort of weird feedback — it didn't hurt to hope, right?

In this case, hope did nothing to help her. Her friend didn't answer, which meant that Lilah would either have to climb over the fence, or abandon Val to who knew what sort of fate. As far as she was concerned, the second option wasn't a real option. She grabbed the chain link fence and looked up, dreading what she was about to do, but seeing no way around it.

She had just hoisted herself up the first few feet when she heard the crunching of a car's wheels on the gravel drive behind her. Letting herself drop to the ground, she brushed her hands off on her pants and tried to look innocent as a large pickup truck rolled into view. She couldn't have been more shocked when Reid got out of the driver's side of the truck, followed by Greg on the other side. What on earth were they doing here?

"Are you all right?" Reid asked, approaching her swiftly with a look of intense worry on his face. Lilah could only nod and look blankly between him and Greg. "Margie called me shortly after you left her house. She seemed to think that you were about to do something heroic and dangerous, and might need backup."

"Oh. You were at work?"

He nodded. "I asked Greg to tag along, just in case we needed the extra help."

Reid was Greg's boss, so Lilah figured that made sense. She realized that she owed Greg an apology for thinking he was a murderer, but that could wait. Right now, they had to help Val.

She caught them up to speed quickly, finishing with, "She's still not answering her phone. She could be hurt somewhere in there, and she needs my help."

The two men eyed the fence, then teamed up to give her a boost over it. She had a terrifying moment at the top, where she was certain that she was going to fall, but somehow managed to cling to the metal links and lower herself safely to the ground on the other side. Reid and Greg followed a moment later, then looked to her for direction. Lilah realized that she had no idea where her friend might be. The lumberyard was big, and somewhat maze-like. It would take them a long time to search the whole thing, but she didn't see what other choice they had.

"Should we split up?" Reid asked.

"Have you ever seen a horror movie?" she asked. "That's always a bad idea."

He held his hands up in mock defeat, then gestured for her to take the lead. She did, choosing a direction at random. She figured that her friend probably hadn't been too near the main building when she screamed, or else the receptionist would have heard her and gone to investigate. That meant that Val had to be somewhere outside, probably nearer to the back fence.

Their search was a tense one, none of them sure what they were going to find. Each time they rounded a corner, Lilah found herself dreading finding her friend dead. There was still a murderer on the loose, after all.

When they finally found her, it was almost as bad as Lilah had been fearing. Val was slouched against a stack of boards, her head drooping down and bleeding from a cut on her forehead. Reid rushed forward to take her pulse.

"She's alive," he said. Lilah felt her knees go weak with relief.

"What happened?" Greg asked, looking around. "Did something fall on her?"

At that moment, they heard the sound of an electric engine coming from behind another stack of wood and moving their way.

"We've got to move her," Lilah hissed. "It wasn't an accident. Someone did this to her, and now they're coming back."

"You aren't supposed to move someone with a head wound," Reid replied, his voice low. "It could hurt her more." He crouched down next to the unconscious woman and touched her shoulder gently, attempting to wake her.

"Hurry. Whoever it is, is getting closer."

It was too late. One of the lumberyard's electric forklifts rounded the corner. Lilah backed up, eyes darting from her friend to the machine that was rolling ominously towards them.

"Stay behind me," Reid said, standing up and moving in front of her protectively. Not in the mood to argue, she did as she was told. Greg shifted beside her, his eyes wide with fear. She could tell that he wanted to run. In fact, she thought he was on the verge of sprinting away when a frown suddenly creased his forehead. He narrowed his eyes.

"Mom?"

The forklift trundled to a halt a few yards away from them. Lilah watched in shock as Marie Motts poked her head out the side.

"Greg? What are you doing here?"

"I think you're the one that needs to answer that question, Mrs. Motts," Reid said in a firm voice.

"Ma, what's going on?"

Marie hesitated, then got fully out of the forklift. She approached them hesitantly, her eyes darting from her son to Val's unconscious body, then back again. "I — I was just shopping for some materials. Your father wanted to rebuild the gazebo."

"Val said she was with a customer," Lilah said, finding her courage. The older woman didn't seem so frightening now that she was out of the forklift. "That was you, wasn't it?"

"No! I was all the way on the other side of the yard —"

"You've got blood on your shirt, Ma," Greg said, his face pale as he took in the truth. "Don't lie to me. Why did you hurt Val?"

"I... I..." The older woman looked crestfallen. "I was trying to protect you. My boy... That horrid woman was saying you murdered Ellen."

"That's not true," Lilah said. "Teri is the one that killed Ellen. I was just telling Val that Greg was innocent."

"Wait, you thought I killed the woman I loved?" Greg asked, his expression horrified.

"No. Well, sort of. But not really. We can talk about it later," she promised. "Right now we need to get Val to the hospital."

122

"Teri didn't do it either," he said, frowning at her. "She can't have. She was talking to the local news crew the whole time we were setting up, including after Ellen didn't come back from the shop. I remember, because they were right across from us, and I saw her showing them some pictures. I thought it was odd." His frown deepened. "Ma, you hit Val over the head and knocked her out, almost killed her. The police said Ellen died from a blow to the skull. You left right after you sent Ellen to the store, claiming you had to use the bathroom. Where did you really go?"

All eyes fell on the older woman. Lilah drew the connection, and gasped. Ellen had died from an injury just like Val's. Not only that, but she had died in the very store that Marie Motts had worked at for years. And if what Greg was saying was true, then she had no alibi for the time of Ellen's murder.

"Greg dear, you don't want to know, really, do you?" Marie asked timidly. "You said you felt free, not having to deal with that woman any more. Let's just leave it at that."

"No. I want the truth." Greg stepped forward. His hands were shaking as he stared at his mother in disbelief. "Did you kill Ellen, Ma? I want the truth."

The older woman's gaze flicked to the left and right, looking for a way out. Her mouth opened and closed as she struggled to find words. At last, her eyes landed on her son, and she fell to her knees.

"I did it," she admitted in a small voice. "I killed her. Greg, I did it for you. She was horrible to you, and I saw how much you were suffering. I knew you would never leave her on your own — she had you convinced that you couldn't do better. I didn't plan on doing it. I just meant to scare her a little. I followed her into the store after I asked her to go pick up more coffee filters for the booth. I was going to lock her in, make her miss her chance to get in front of the news crew's cameras; that was the whole reason that she agreed to help out in the first place, you know. She thought it would look good if the crews saw her involved with the festival."

"Why did you do it?" her son asked, his voice hoarse.

"Because she started talking about you, saying horrible things! She was just muttering to herself, talking about how she was sick of hearing all about that toy store you dreamed of, and how you were lucky you made good money, or else she would leave you in a heartbeat. I couldn't stand it. I grabbed one of the cast iron pans we had on sale and just hit her with it, as hard as I could. I wasn't thinking, and before I knew it, she was laying on the floor in front of me. Not moving. Dead."

The older woman broke down into sobs. Greg took a step back from her, a look of complete and utter disgust on his face. Lilah felt like she had to throw up. This was worse than she had ever imagined. She looked to Reid, to see how he was taking it, and saw that he had his phone out. Out of all of them, he was the only one who had kept it together enough to call 911.

"The ambulance will be here soon," he said. "The operator heard everything. They're sending a car to pick up Mrs. Motts as well."

Lilah nodded, then closed her eyes, grateful that he had had the presence of mind to make the call. She couldn't look at Greg, whose face was twisted with disbelief, and she didn't want to so much as glance at Marie. Instead, she crouched down next to Val and took her friend's limp hand in her own.

"It's okay," she told her. "Help will be here soon. Just hold on, Val. Hold on."

CHAPTER SIXTEEN

"I can't believe I missed all of that."

"Trust me. I wish I hadn't been there. You're a lot better off without those horrible memories," Lilah said.

She watched her friend carefully. Val had been released from the hospital only yesterday. To celebrate her recovery, Margie had offered to pay for a meal for all of them at the diner. She had, of course, invited Reid along. The handsome business man was currently sitting across from Lilah, though his eyes, too, were on Valerie.

"That's quite the bruise she gave you," he said. "I'm surprised they let you out already."

"I'm hard-headed," Val said. "It must not be just a turn of phrase in my case."

Lilah smiled. If her friend was joking already, then she really must be feeling all right.

"There's just one thing I'm still curious about," the other woman continued. "Teri. What in the world was she doing with all of those photos of Ellen?"

"Why don't we ask her?" Margie said, turning to look across the diner where the woman in question was sitting alone, looking dejected.

They waved Teri over. She came reluctantly, looking confused and embarrassed at all of the ruckus. Reid got up and squeezed into the booth next to Lilah, so Teri would have more space across from them.

"What's going on?" she asked, glancing at each of them in turn, her expression wary.

"I found this in your booth the other day," Lilah said, deciding that being straightforward was the best way to go. She pulled the now somewhat crumpled folder out of her purse and handed it to the other woman.

"Ah." Teri took the folder, embarrassment causing her cheeks to flame. "I guess you want to know why I have all of this stuff?"

All four of them nodded.

"Right. Well, first let me say I'm not proud of it. A couple of weeks ago, Ellen and I tried out for the same part in a hairspray commercial. I thought I had the part in the bag. Ellen *always* lost out to me. But then she got the part. It was horrible, I was so embarrassed, and to make matters worse, she kept taunting me about it. When I heard she was coming back to town for the festival, I convinced her assistant to forward me her schedule. I followed her around and took a bunch of pictures of her. I kept all of the worst ones. That day in the salon, that was golden. Then, when the news crew came to report on the Arts and Crafts Festival, I gave them a bunch of the pictures and told them what a terrible person she was. The media loves embarrassing stuff like that, you know? I figured she could do with some bad publicity. But then, after she died, I felt terrible. I kept looking back over everything I had done, wondering how on earth I could have been so petty." Teri shook her head sadly. "Like I said, I'm not proud of it."

Val snorted, but quickly covered it up by faking a cough. "Don't beat yourself up too much. She would have done the same to you in a heartbeat, and we all know it."

"Yeah. I suppose you're right." Teri gave them a small smile. "I feel better telling you guys all of that. It felt like some horrible secret I was doomed to carry around forever."

"Trust me, compared to what we thought, it's nothing," Val said seriously. "Lilah here was convinced that you were the killer."

It was Lilah's turn to blush. "Yeah. Um, sorry about that. I went through a phase where I thought I wanted to be a private investigator, and I started trying to solve the case of Ellen's death. It turns out I'm about as good at detective work as I was at being a hairdresser."

"So in other words, terrible. Unless we want a terrible dye job, then you're our girl," her friend said with a grin.

"That about sums it up," Lilah said, laughing. She felt more lighthearted than she had since she got fired from the hair salon. "I think for now I'll stick to waitressing and helping Margie out with her cookies. Everything else I try seems to end in disaster, and I've had enough of those... for this week, at least."

Made in the USA
Monee, IL
30 January 2022

90174152R00075